To Susan
From Mom
2014

The Stable

Sharon Feldt

Abbott Press books may be ordered through booksellers or by contacting:

Abbott Press
1663 Liberty Drive
Bloomington, IN 47403
www.abbottpress.com
Phone: 1-866-697-5310

ISBN: 978-1-4582-1666-3 (hc)
ISBN: 978-1-4582-1664-9 (sc)
ISBN: 978-1-4582-1665-6 (e)

Library of Congress Control Number: 2014910405

Printed in the United States of America.

Abbott Press rev. date: 10/08/2014

For Birdie, who loved Christmas best of all.

Acknowledgments

There are so many who have helped bring this story to life:

JM & LF, who are my unofficial "editor in chief"; Author Jim Ainsworth, who has given so generously of his time and expertise, Mary Brooke Casad, children's book author and friend, who lent an ear numerous times over lunch and choir practice; The Ladies of Bright Star Literary Society (Terry, Carol, Wilma, the Jans, Patti, Pat, JoAnn, Jane, Mary , Linda and Miss Elizabeth) who are my personal literary inspirations: JS, SG, PS and DW who have given their professional thumbs up to it over a glorious beach weekend; and of course, my lovely husband John, without whom I would have no springboard off which to bounce! Thank you. Love you all.

Tags

"The Christmas Story as told by the animals, who offered their very best for the Holy family."
-Terry Mathews, arts editor, *Sulphur Springs News-Telegram*

"A story repeated through the ages told by a distinctive, entertaining, and ispiring new voice."
-Jim Ainsworth, author, *The Rivers Trilogy,*
Biscuits Across the Brazos and *Home Light Burning*

"This fresh perspective on an ancient story speaks to the hearts of children of all ages: Sharon Feldt's beautiful retelling of the Christmas story brings a new appreciation of all God's creatures who celebrated the birth of Jesus."
-Mary Brooke Casad, children's book author
Bluebonnet the Armadillo Series

The village was bustling with activity.

An atmosphere of excitement filled the air.

Visitors were arriving from other towns, and families were opening their homes to welcome friends and relatives.

The King had declared that all people of the land should return to villages where they had been born to register for the census.

Even the animals were stirring with anticipation.

On a road outside the village, a man and his wife travelling from Nazareth stopped for a rest. The donkey on which the woman rode sensed something special about this trip. As he grazed in the grass, close by a field mouse nibbled on a barley stalk.

“Where are you going?” asked the mouse.

“To Bethlehem”, said the donkey.

“You must be very tired carrying the woman and those bundles. She is very large!”

“I’m made to help my master”, replied the donkey. “And the woman is not heavy. She is carrying a child soon to be born.”

“I have been to Bethlehem”, said the mouse. “It is full of people. More come into the village each hour.”

The donkey spoke. “We cannot move too quickly because of the woman. I am trying to walk gently.”

The man walked to the donkey and attached the lead rope. He strapped on the bundles of belongings and helped the woman onto the donkey's back.

As they continued their journey, the woman sang softly. It was a beautiful melody, and very pleasing to the donkey's ears. The woman had a calm and kind nature, as did the man. They spoke softly to one another about the baby that was to be born. The donkey knew from their conversations that the child would be well loved and cared for.

Arriving in the village the travelers encountered a mass of people, livestock and belongings. As the man went from inn to inn, he found all the rooms taken. But at the last stop, the innkeeper, seeing that the woman was about to give birth, offered them a place in the stable. It was a large cave in the rock, a warm safe area where grain was stored and the animals were given shelter. As the man began unloading the belongings, the donkey spied the little field mouse at the back of the stable area by the grain.

“This is no place for the woman”, scolded the mouse. “And certainly not suitable for a baby!”

The donkey sighed. “Yes, but it is all they could find. At least it is dry and warm.”

The mouse scurried away and the donkey watched as he scampered from stall to stall whispering to the other animals. There were two cows, a ewe and her lambs, three geese, two hens and an ox. Above them in a niche in the rock, a great barn owl quietly observed the scene below.

The man had pulled some of the hay into a soft pile so the woman could rest. She lay back gently and began the soft singing as she had done on the journey. The man surveyed the contents of the stable and found two wooden mangers, one filled with fresh hay for the animals and another empty. He pulled the empty one close to where the woman lay. The sweet singing subsided as the woman fell asleep. The man covered her with a woolen blanket and left the stable to register for the census.

Suddenly there was a flurry of activity among the animals. The geese began gathering up feathers and down from the stalls. The ox and cows began nudging clean hay toward the manger. The ewe and her lambs sat quietly as the hens used their beaks to pull loose pieces of wool from their backs. Quietly, as the woman slept, the animals filled the empty manger with clean hay, soft feathers and wool. At least this child would have a soft place to lay its head. The warm breath of the ox and cows filled the stable, soothing the sleeping woman.

Above the great owl watched with wise eyes. "WHOOO? WHOOO?" he softly wondered.

As day faded into night, the animals were amazed that the little manger remained bathed in a beautiful, soft light, for there was no lantern in the the stable, no hearth for a fire, and outside the night was darkening. But inside, the woman's face shone.

When the man returned he prepared bread and fruit for the woman to eat. The donkey lay down close to his master, staring at the face of the woman. Yes, something about her was very special.

Suddenly the woman said quietly, "It is time. Prepare the swaddling cloths. Our son is about to be born."

The man hurriedly pulled the cloths from the bundles. The child was born. The animals watched with wonder as the mother gently wrapped her son in strips of cloth, binding him and cradling him to her. She resumed her soothing song. The man and woman looked at one another and then gazed lovingly at the newborn infant. The child's face was beautiful, glowing as his mother sang. There was a serenity about him, a peacefulness that filled the stable.

Outside the village something was happening. The little field mouse scurried to see. His eyes widened as he saw a single brilliant star shining down on the stable. He watched the shepherds from the fields move toward the village, while above an angel beckoned them onward. It was truly a night of miracles!

The little mouse scampered back inside and the donkey watched as his little friend raced from stall to stall whispering to the other animals. The great owl, observing the activity below, looked at the child and again wondered, "WHOOO? WHOOO?"

As the shepherds came into the stable, they knelt before the child. The animals watched as the people bowed down to this tiny baby and called him Savior.

The man and woman did not seem surprised by this behavior. They smiled and kissed the child, calling him Jesus, Son of the Most High.

The donkey nuzzled the woman and watched the baby, whose face mirrored purity and love. The mouse snuggled in a corner of the manger wanting to be close to the tiny child.

The great owl, no longer wondering, looked down on the infant and with bowed head, simply whispered, "Lord".

All things bright and beautiful,
All creatures great and small,
All things wise and wonderful:
The Lord God made them all.
Hymns for Little Children
Cecil F. Alexander,
1848

CPSIA information can be obtained at www.ICGtesting.com
Printed in the USA
BVOW10*0615081114

374231BV00001B/1/P